If the World Ran Out of B's

Written by Samantha & Bill Shireman

Illustrated by Dean Stanton

BEYOND
WORDS
Publishing
I N C

Beyond Words Publishing, Inc.
20827 N.W. Cornell Road, Suite 500
Hillsboro, Oregon 97124-9808
503-531-8700
1-800-284-9673

Editor: Michelle Roehm McCann
Design: Dean Stanton

Printed in Belgium
Distributed to the book trade by Publishers Group West

Library of Congress Cataloging-in-Publication Data

Shireman, Samantha
If the world ran out of B's / by Samantha and Bill Shireman ; illustrated by Dean Stanton.
p. cm.
Summary: Explores what would happen if people used up the limited supplies of the
letter B, with such results as Bill becoming ill, and children opening gift oxes.
ISBN 1-58270-059-1
[1. Alphabet—Fiction. 2. Humorous stories. 3. Stories in rhyme.] I. Shireman, William K.
II. Stanton, Dean, ill. III. Title.

PZ8.3.S5567 If 2002
[E]—dc21

2001035465

The corporate mission of Beyond Words Publishing, Inc.:
    Inspire to Integrity

People use **B's** just the way
that they please . . .

They think they can always get more B's with ease.

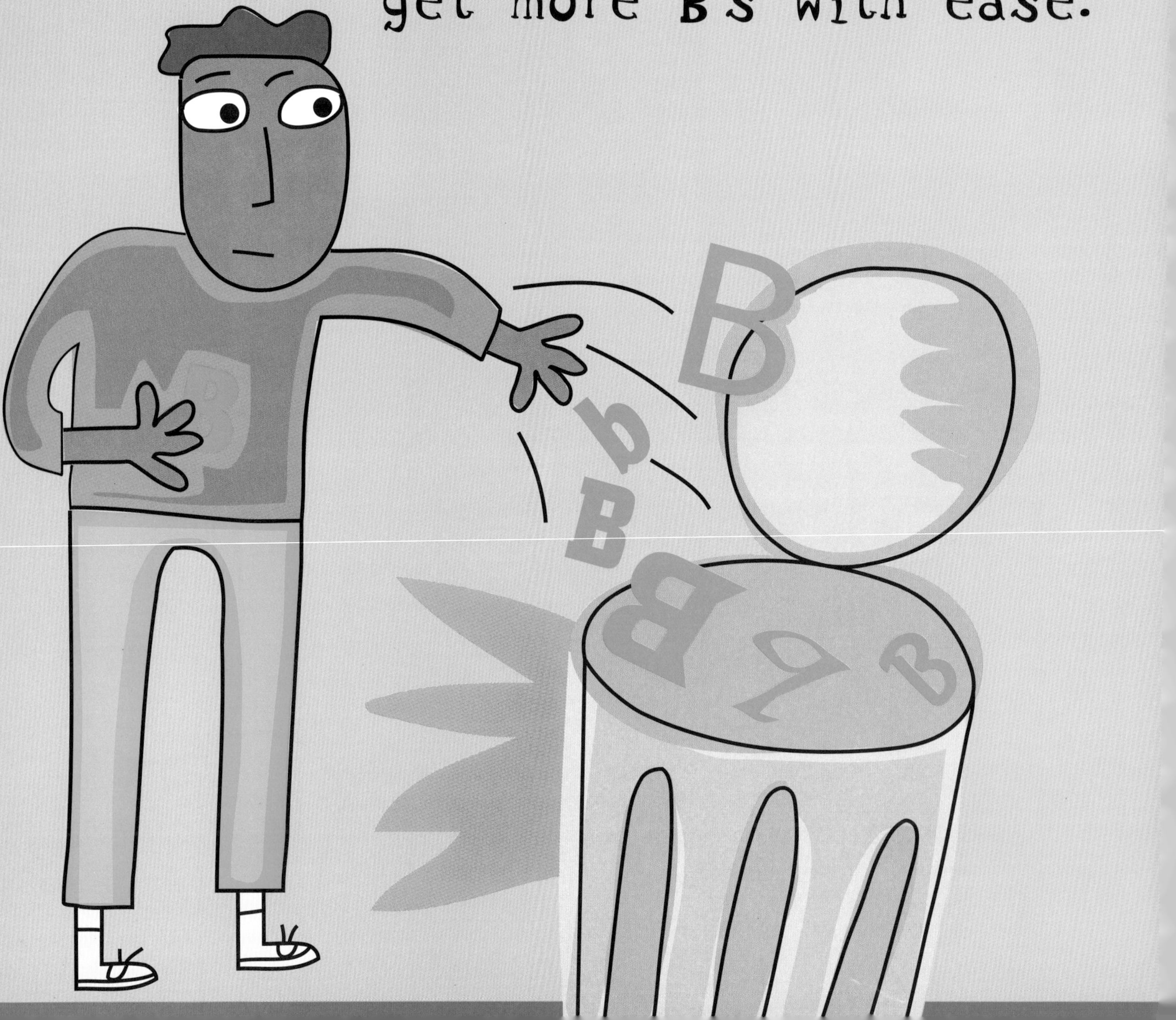

But the world has only
so many B's.

They don't, after all,
just grow back on trees.

If we all
cavalierly
toss B's
about,

eventually the world would totally run out!

That would be trouble, for as you will see, the world just can't get along without B's.

Without B's,
Bill would
be ill.

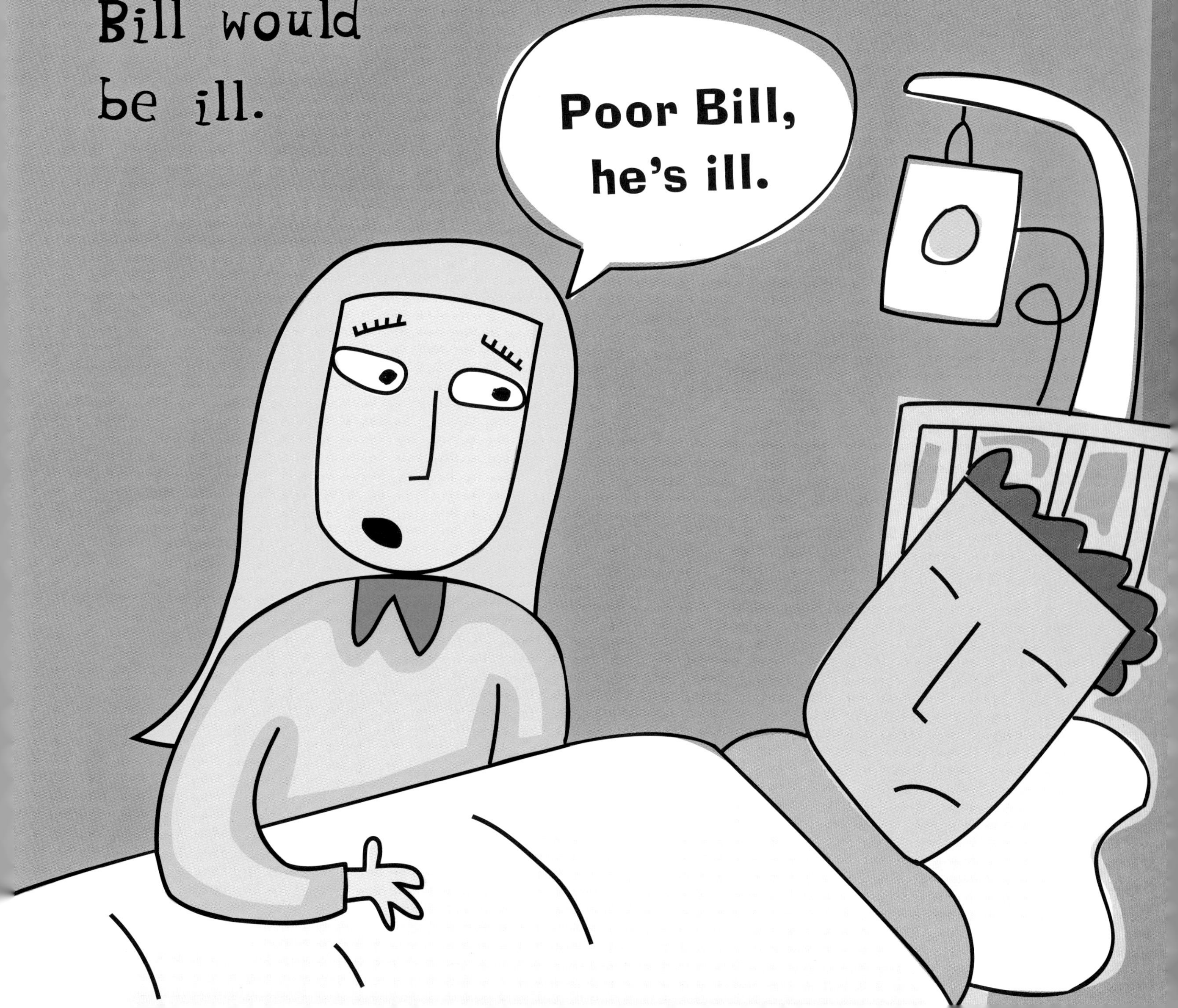

No one would know where a bat was at.

And kids who wanted bicycles would just get icycles.

When it was time for Bob and Ed
to go to bed...

o should go to his ed,
and Ed to Ed's ed.

And if you wanted to climb a tree, you'd be careful of getting stung by an e!

No one would ever win at bingo, 'cause all they could yell at the end would be Ingo!

And kids getting presents wouldn't open their boxes.

They'd have to unwrap and unpackage their oxes.

Halloween ghosts couldn't scare you with boo! They'd just have to say...

Dogs couldn't have barked to get onto the Ark.

And if the bug bit them, it wouldn't be just an itty-bitty bug bite, it'd be an itty-itty ug ite.

And you'd have no brain to stay out of the rain.

Grooms would always forget to bring the **oh-so-important** wedding ring.

So instead of a bride,
he'd just get a ride.

Everyone's birthday would happen on irthday.

But don't
be too worried 'bout using
all your B's.
Because the B's are an
IDEA, you can use
all you please.
Be clever in B use and
believe me you'll see
that your B's will
always be
bountiful...

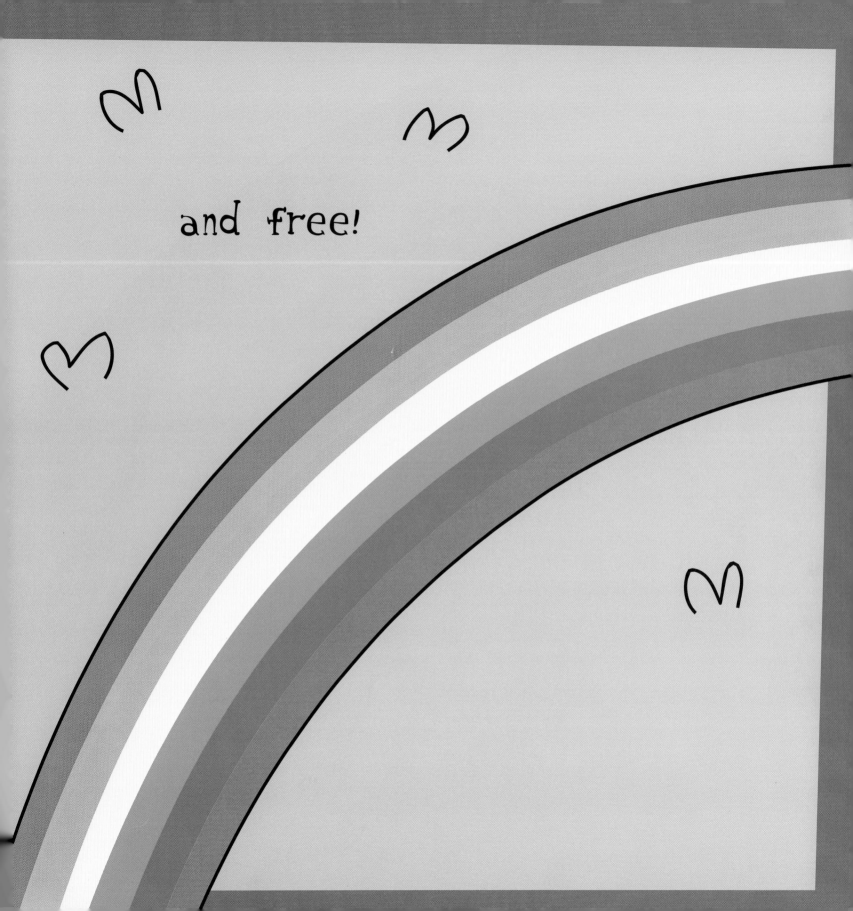

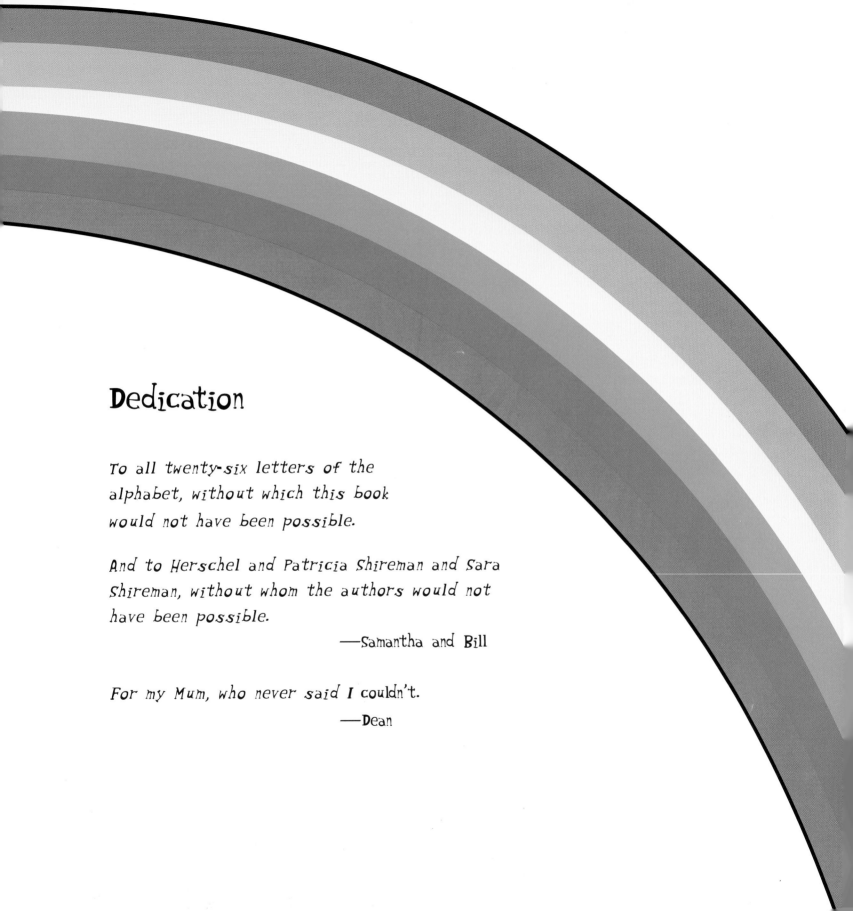

Dedication

*To all twenty-six letters of the
alphabet, without which this book
would not have been possible.*

*And to Herschel and Patricia Shireman and Sara
Shireman, without whom the authors would not
have been possible.*

—Samantha and Bill

For my Mum, who never said I couldn't.

—Dean